Witch's Wishes

VIVIAN VANDE VELDE

Holiday House / New York

Happy wishes
to my friends
at Iroquois School

Library of Congress Cataloging-in-Publication Data

Vande Velde, Vivian.
    Witch's wishes / by Vivian Vande Velde.—1st ed.
      p. cm.
    Summary: On Halloween, six-year-old Sarah encounters a witch who
repays her kindness by making her magic wand real for the night,
resulting in a series of wishes come true that the witch then has to fix.
    ISBN 0-8234-1789-1
    [1. Witches—Fiction. 2. Halloween—Fiction. 3. Wishes—Fiction.]
  I. Title.

PZ7.V2773 Wht 2003
[Fic]—dc21

                                         2002191915

Contents

CHAPTER 1
The Witching Hour

One All Hallows' Eve, as winter chased summer around the last corner of the year and leaves were crisp and orange and yellow, the old witch woke up from her afternoon nap and knew that something was wrong. She realized by the dimming light that the sun was just setting, which meant she had overslept.

"Oh, *why* didn't I get that alarm clock fixed?" she moaned as she leaped out of bed and began to search in her closet for her party dress.

"Because you're cheap," her magic broom said from its corner. "It's been grinding and squeaking and losing time all week. *Anybody* else would have had it fixed or bought a new one. Or you could have fixed it yourself with a magic spell, but you're also lazy."

"Oh, hush," the witch told the broom. "*You* could have called out to me."

"Not my job," the broom said. "I notice you aren't criticizing your new pet goldfish for not waking you."

The witch didn't point out that being a goldfish, Sweet Pea couldn't talk. The broom was just sulking from being a bit jealous—sort of like sibling rivalry, though not exactly.

The witch found her party dress—it was black, as all her official witch dresses were, but it was satin. Luckily, she had remembered to pick it up earlier in the week from the dry cleaner. And she found her good boots—they were under her bed, never put away from the autumnal equinox "Remember the '70s" Disco Night Dance. She mussed her hair because it was looking too neat from having been slept on.

"Why tonight?" she muttered as she pasted a wart to her nose (since warts were only worn on formal occasions, they weren't worth the trouble of growing), but as soon as the words were out of her mouth, she warned the broom, "I wasn't talking to you."

The broom answered anyway: "Of course not. Just consider me a convenience. Don't worry. I'm used to it."

Tonight was the witches' All Hallows' Eve Ghastly Gala A-go-go (with a '60s theme, of course), at the Irondequoit Senior Center, where the witches were more senior than anybody else there ever imagined. The witch was on the refreshments committee and was supposed to have the mulled cider ready for when the doors officially opened at midnight. (Thank goodness others were in charge of supplying the snacks and cookies! Half the witches were on some or another kind of diet: low sodium, high fiber, no sugar—but they got cranky if their goodies tasted like diet food. And nobody likes a cranky witch—especially other cranky witches.) Now here it was, who knew what time, but dark enough for the neighborhood streetlights to be on. To make matters worse, the best cider is cider that has been mulled a long time, and she hadn't even bought any yet.

She turned on the living room light because she hated coming home to a dark house. "See you later, Sweet Pea," she called to her pet goldfish, whom she kept in her witch's cauldron because she felt pet store fish tanks were too confining.

The only good thing, the witch thought, was that she wouldn't have to come back to change after going to the supermarket. All Hallows' Eve is the night most folk call Halloween, and many people would be dressed up. Everyone would assume she was wearing a Halloween costume, with her black dress, tall laced boots, and pointed hat—she found the hat where it had fallen behind the couch, where she'd set it on top of a teddy bear specifically so that she *could* find it.

She knew she should take her car, a powder blue minivan, but it was almost out of gas, and she would lose more time going to the gas station. Or she could walk, at least to the supermarket. Witches have a rule not to ride their broomsticks till an hour past sunset to lessen the chances of being seen. And, in case she could have forgotten, her broom reminded her: "Not dark enough for flying."

But she was running so late she convinced herself that no one would see her.

And that was how the old witch came to almost collide with the Channel 12 air traffic report helicopter.

CHAPTER 2
Oops!

The old witch's eyes were bedazzled by the lights of the supermarket's parking lot, so she didn't see the helicopter till the last moment.

It was only when her broom asked "Are we going to ram him or just scare the socks off him?" that she became aware she and a helicopter were about to occupy the same space at the same time. They were close enough that she could see the helicopter pilot's open mouth and bugging-out eyes.

Immediately the witch pushed down on the broomstick. She and her magic broom went into a dive. There was little time for fancy maneuvering, and she certainly didn't want to give the pilot a chance to track her, so she aimed straight for the open Dumpster behind the supermarket.

The landing was rough and smelly.

"Oh, thanks," the broom said. "I haven't had so much fun since last summer when you ran over me with the lawn mower."

"Shhh!" the witch hissed. She cast a quick spell, making a spotlight that projected an image of a witch into the sky.

The helicopter hovered for almost a minute, but the pilot must eventually have convinced himself that he had been startled by a Halloween decoration.

The witch ended the spell and tried to swing her legs over the edge of the Dumpster. But she wasn't as young as she had been.

As a matter of fact, nobody is.

Still, at 107 years old—even though she didn't look a day over eighty—she was farther away from young than most. Her bones creaked, the arm she was leaning on slipped off a rotten head of lettuce, and she ended up sprawled on her back, gazing at the sky.

"That's not snickering I'm hearing, is it?" she asked.

"Absolutely not," the broom assured her.

She dug the shaft end of the broom as far into the garbage as she could, which was only partially to get leverage. The Dumpster was filled with lumpy, irregularly shaped plastic bags—some more solid than others, many of them leaky, all of them slippery. It took her quite a bit of effort to make her way to the edge, and once she did get there, she sat with her legs dangling over the side, huffing mightily, her dress pulled well up over her hairy, saggy knees.

"Uh-oh," the broom said.

The old witch waited for a snide remark about people who don't shave their legs just because they plan on wearing a long dress. But when the broom didn't say anything else, she looked around.

And saw two kids standing on the pavement, staring up at her.

The little girl looked about six, and she was in a pink taffeta top, pink tutu, and pink tights. The old witch would have taken her for a ballerina, except for the wings, sequin tiara, and stick with a star and tinsel streamers on top that was evidently meant to be a magic wand. The girl was obviously dressed as a fairy princess—a fairy princess carrying a flashlight to see by and a pillowcase to carry the Halloween treats she extorted from neighborhood residents.

Her brother—he had to be her brother because he was at least eleven years old and no eleven-year-old boy would go trick-or-treating with a six-year-old girl unless their mother made him—also had a pillowcase for collecting goodies. In addition, he had slicked-back hair, a cape, and fangs. Either he was meant to be the "Before" picture on the poster of a demented orthodontist, or he was dressed as a vampire.

Uh-oh, the witch thought. Witnesses.

The broom started to say, "Now you've—" but the witch interrupted, whispering a warning to it from between clenched teeth: "No talking in public."

The little girl spoke. She said in a tone of awe, "Justin. Look. It's a witch."

"Yeah, right, Sarah." The boy—Justin—spoke in a sarcastic, superior voice as he shone his flashlight directly into the old witch's face. "It's just some old bag lady."

Bag lady? the witch thought, squinting to avoid the glare. This is my best dress. It's a Liz

Claiborne, and I didn't even wait until it was on sale to buy it.

"She's a witch," Sarah insisted. "She fell out of the sky." Then, addressing the witch, she asked, "Did that hurt?"

Well, the girl was right, but it was safer to pretend the boy was. As though she were content to stay there all night, the old witch leaned back onto the black plastic bag that smelled of overripe bananas and oranges and potatoes that the store's produce manager was discarding.

The boy tugged on his sister's shoulder. "Come on, let's get out of here."

But the girl, even though she looked afraid, stepped closer. "*Are* you hurt?" she asked the old witch. Then she said, "Wait a minute."

"Sarah," Justin urged his sister, "what are you doing?"

What *was* she doing? The old witch saw the girl was rummaging around in her pillowcase. Finally, from beneath what she had gathered so far this evening, Sarah pulled out a white plastic purse. No well-dressed fairy princess should leave home without her white plastic purse, even if she has to carry it in the bottom of a pillowcase. The old witch waited while the girl poked around in her purse.

"Sarah." Again the boy tried to pull her away, but this time she squirmed loose and ran up to the Dumpster.

"Here." The girl was handing something up to her. A stick of gum? No. "It's a glow-in-the-dark Prom Night Barbie Band-Aid," the girl explained. "They make you heal even faster than regular Band-Aids."

From his safer distance, as though he thought his sister could hear but the old witch could not, the boy hissed, "Sarah, don't get so close—she might have something catching."

Rotten little kid, the old witch thought. But the girl was sweet. "Thank you," the witch said. She opened the package and wrapped the Band-Aid around her finger. "Feeling better already," she assured the girl.

The boy came and grabbed his sister by the arm, causing her to drop her pillowcase onto the ground.

"Justin," Sarah complained as a couple candy bars rolled out.

"Leave them," Justin ordered, just barely giving her time to pick up the pillowcase.

The girl turned to wave good-bye just before they got to the corner.

The witch waved back.

Once they were gone, the witch climbed out of the Dumpster. She used a spell to give herself a soft landing.

"Didn't I try to warn you?" the broom asked. "But can you ever be bothered to take advice from the household appliances? Oh, no, not you."

Ignoring the broom, the witch said another spell to clean herself off. This wasn't as effective as dry cleaning, but it was the best she could do for the moment.

And now for that shopping. . . .

"Cider, cinnamon," she reminded herself as she went around the front to enter the supermarket. There had been three things the preparation committee had asked her to bring. What was that third one? Ginger? Allspice? No, all three started with *c*, which had made them— she had thought—easy to remember. Cocoa? Cream of tartar? She didn't think so, but was sure the right one would come back to her when she rested a bit. Doing spells was tiring, and she had just done three in about two minutes.

She saw the boy, still tugging on his sister's arm, going up the sidewalk of the house beyond the supermarket.

Such a kind little girl. She made a very cute little fairy princess, with her fake crown and her fake wings and . . .

The witch thought of a fine way to thank the girl for her kindness. She went for one more spell, and made the girl's toy wand a real magic wand—just for tonight.

"Are you sure that's wise?" the broom demanded, a hysterical edge to its voice.

"No talking in public," the witch reminded, and she walked into the supermarket, the automatic doors opening for her.

CHAPTER 3
Witch Wish #1

Sarah told Justin, "You're walking too fast. You're going to make me fall."

"It would serve you right," Justin answered. "And then I could bring you back home and go out with my friends instead of my baby sister. What's the matter with you? Talking to a stranger—to a bag lady! That's just dumb."

"I wish you'd be nice to me," Sarah muttered.

Justin stopped so suddenly, Sarah bumped into him. She thought he must be angry for what she'd said, and now he'd be angrier still that she'd plowed right into him.

"You're absolutely right," Justin said. "I've been a real jerk. I'm sorry."

Sarah waited for the punch line to her brother's joke.

Instead, he said, "Rick and Eric and Shane can get along without me. This is actually kind of fun, you and me together. It reminds me of when I was a little kid and Halloween seemed like a magical night when anything could happen."

Sarah looked at her brother suspiciously. "What do you want?" she demanded.

"Ouch," Justin said, acting as though her words hurt him. He reached into his pillowcase and pulled out a handful of candy, which he dumped into her bag without even checking to see whether it was stuff he liked. "I'm sorry I made you drop that candy back there behind the store," he said.

By then they had reached the door of the first house after the store. For a change, Justin let Sarah ring the doorbell. When the woman who lived there opened the door, Justin stepped back so that she could see Sarah first, and he didn't do his corny "I vant to drink your blood" routine before Sarah had a chance to say "Trick or treat."

"Oh, aren't you cute," the woman told both

of them. She had a bowl of suckers and she asked, "Red, green, yellow, or purple?"

"Red," Sarah and Justin answered together.

"Oh, dear, there's only one red one left," the woman said, pawing through the bowl.

"That's okay," Justin said. "Give that one to my sister. I can take a green one."

Green? Sarah thought. *Justin is taking a green sucker?*

When the woman closed the door, Justin turned to go. "What's the matter?" he asked, seeing Sarah standing on the stoop holding the red sucker.

"Don't you want to trade?" she asked.

He looked at the green sucker in his hand. "Did you change your mind?" he asked.

Carefully, she said, "No."

He dropped the green sucker into her bag. "Keep them both," he said.

Slowly, because she still suspected a trick, she said, "Thank you."

"You're welcome," he said.

Weird, Sarah thought.

They made their way down the street, house after house, with Justin being nice to her. Then, at the farthest house before they would have to turn back home, a man opened the door and a dog jumped out at them.

Startled, Sarah squealed, and Justin immediately put himself between the dog and Sarah.

"That's okay," the man said. "Daisy's just saying hello. She wouldn't hurt you. Get down, Daisy."

Sarah saw that Daisy was wagging her tail and trying to lick Justin.

"Down," Daisy's owner repeated, and the dog lay down. She was mostly, though not entirely, a Labrador retriever, and she didn't look nearly so big now that she was still.

Sarah came out from behind Justin.

The owner said, "Don't be afraid. She won't bite."

Justin was petting her. "She's soft," he told Sarah.

Hesitantly, Sarah put her hand out. Daisy licked it, which tickled. When Sarah touched her golden fur, it *was* soft.

From the other room came a whimper, then a bang, then the sound of nails skittering on the floor.

"Uh-oh," the owner said, although he didn't really sound worried. "The puppies knocked the gate down again."

In another moment, seven puppies came running through the house toward them. Because Daisy was lying across the doorway, the man couldn't close the door and keep them in, so they swarmed onto the stoop, over Daisy, sniffing and licking at Sarah and Justin.

"Oh, they're so cute," Sarah said.

"Want one?" the man asked. "We're looking for homes for them."

Wow! Sarah thought.

But Justin shook his head. "We already have a dog," he told the man.

"But Dudley is *your* dog," Sarah protested, for Dudley never paid any attention to Sarah, just Justin and his goofy friends.

Justin shrugged.

"I want a dog of my own," Sarah said.

"Ask Mom," Justin told her. "I'll bring you back here if she says yes."

"Everyone should have a dog," Sarah said. "I wish everyone did."

"Listen," the man said, "why don't you take one of the puppies home to show your mom? If she says no, then you can bring the pup back." He winked at Sarah. "It'll be easier to talk her into it if you already have one."

Sarah nodded, and Justin didn't argue.

Sarah chose a white-and-golden-colored puppy that looked like a smaller version of Daisy. "I'm going to call her Maxine," Sarah said, because that struck her as a very sophisticated name.

The man put Maxine in a cardboard box along with a bag of dog food and a bowl for water.

Justin asked her, "Do you want me to carry the puppy or the pillowcase of candy?"

"The candy please," Sarah said. She wasn't even afraid that he'd keep it once he got hold of it.

Justin walked patiently beside her, even though it took them quite a while because the box was bulky and she kept having to stop to rest—and to check to make sure Maxine was still there. Justin shone his flashlight on the sidewalk in front of Sarah so that she could see where she was going without danger of tripping.

Other trick-or-treaters were farther down the street, squealing in excitement. Two kids, dressed like the front and back ends of a cow, came running down the sidewalk, each carrying a squirming bundle of fur. "Puppies!" one of them called out to Sarah and Justin. "The people at number five-three-seven are giving away puppies."

"Yeah," Justin called after them, "so's six-oh-one."

But neither half of the cow slowed down or answered.

"This is such fun. I love Halloween," Sarah said. "I wish every day was Halloween."

Justin said, "I don't think anybody older than six could handle the strain," but he smiled while he said it.

And so Sarah and Justin continued down the street, and around the corner, to their own house.

"Trick or treat," Sarah called as Justin held the door for her.

"Thank goodness you're home," their mother called from the kitchen. "The oddest thing happened. Look what I found."

Sarah walked into the kitchen, still holding her box with Daisy's puppy in it.

Their mother was sitting on the kitchen floor, wearing the Little Bo Peep costume in which she'd been greeting the trick-or-treaters. But instead of a toy sheep, she was holding a puppy of her own.

CHAPTER 4
Puppy Love

"Hey!" Justin said. "Where'd the puppy come from?"

"I don't know," Mom answered. Sitting on the floor in her Little Bo Peep costume, Mom looked younger than Sarah was used to. "We were running low on candy, so I sent your father to the store to get more, but meanwhile I came into the kitchen to see if there was anything else I could be giving away, and here the little guy was." The little guy was a terrier.

"Guess what?" Sarah said. She put the box down on the floor so that her mother could see Daisy's puppy, Maxine.

Inside the box, Maxine started jumping at the side, trying to get out.

The terrier puppy wriggled away from Mom and balanced on his hind legs, trying to see inside the box.

"Oh, dear," Mom said. "Where did you get that?"

"Some man gave her to me as a Halloween treat," Sarah said.

"That wasn't a very responsible thing to do," Mom complained. "He had no right to do such a thing without checking to see if it was all right with the family."

"He said we could bring her back if you said so," Sarah said. "But can't I keep her, please? Her name is Maxine. She's a very well-behaved puppy, and I promise to take care of her and feed her and walk her and clean up her poop."

Justin chimed in with support. "I can help Sarah take care of her," he said.

"That's not the point," Mom said. Both puppies were standing up, sniffing at each other over the edge of the box. "We already have Dudley . . ."

At the sound of his name, Justin's dog began whimpering and scratching at the basement door.

Mom continued, "Who I locked up because I didn't know how he would react to this one.

But two puppies! At least we know where yours comes from, so we can return her."

"Oh, but, Mom," Sarah said, "I already promised Maxine she could stay."

Just then, they heard Dad's car pull into the driveway.

"We'll discuss this in a minute," Mom said, using her shepherd's crook to scramble to her feet.

Dad came in through the side door. He was wearing white woolly pants and a white woolly sweatshirt because he was supposed to be Little Bo Peep's lost sheep. But he had his mask pushed up on top of his head, and he was saying, "You'll never guess what happened. While I was in the grocery store, someone abandoned . . ." He stopped, looking at the puppy on the kitchen floor and the other puppy in the box. He looked down at the third puppy in his arms. Slowly he finished, "A puppy in the backseat of our car." This one was such a combination of breeds, it was impossible to call it any one thing—besides cute.

"Yay!" Sarah cried. "A dog for each of us! A dog for everybody!" She paused for a moment, considering—realizing that not fifteen minutes ago she had wished for exactly that.

"Some of these puppies will have to go back," Mom said.

"Back where?" Dad asked. "I can't drive back to the grocery store and just toss this little fellow out into the parking lot."

"Well, no," Mom agreed. "But I don't know where mine came from either."

"Let's keep them all," Sarah said. "They'll be company for each other and for Dudley."

"Dudley doesn't need that much company," Mom said.

"We wouldn't want them to end up at the pound," Justin pointed out.

Mom answered, "That's why we definitely need to start by returning the one whose owner we know."

"No fair!" Sarah protested. "I can keep Maxine in my room. I'll take care of her. You won't even know she's there."

"Sarah—," Dad started, but she could tell by his tone of voice that he wasn't going to agree with her, so she wailed, "Why not? Why do I have to give up my puppy while you all get to keep yours?"

"We probably won't keep any of them," Dad said, which was even worse.

"But I can take care of mine. She won't be

any trouble. When I go to school, I can bring her with me. She'll be good and she won't bark or chew on things or anything. Will you, Maxine?"

Maxine licked her face, which Sarah took to be as good as a promise.

"Sarah," Mom said in her quiet but no-nonsense voice, "you're not being reasonable."

That's what her parents always said. When Justin got mad at her, he called her a dummy; when her parents told her she wasn't reasonable, that was the parent—polite—way of saying the same thing.

She picked Maxine up and stamped her feet all the way down the hall to her room. "I am *not* an unreasonable dummy," she muttered to herself. She was smart enough to take care of a puppy. She knew she was. "I wish people thought I was smart," she grumbled. Then they'd let her keep the puppy. For good measure, she added, "I wish my parents would let me keep Maxine."

"Young lady," her mother called after her, "don't you dare stamp your feet and slam your door. You get back here until we finish talking with you."

Sarah stamped her feet all the way back up the hall.

"I don't know," her father was saying to her mother, "maybe she *is* grown-up enough to have her own dog."

Sarah immediately stopped stamping her feet so that she would appear more grown-up.

Her mother had her hands on her hips. "Well, of course she is," Mom told Dad. "That's what I called her back to say: *Sarah you may keep the dog.*"

"Thank you, thank you." Sarah ran to hug Mom despite the fact that Maxine was still in her arms.

"Yay!" Justin cheered.

Mom patted Sarah on the head, then—with a giving-in sigh—she patted Maxine, too.

Sarah went to give her father a hug, but someone was knocking on the door, and he turned to answer that.

Mom glanced at the clock on the stove. "I'd have thought it was getting late for trick-or-treaters," she said.

But it wasn't a trick-or-treater—not at all.

CHAPTER 5
Nothing to Sneeze At

It wasn't a trick-or-treater that their father let into the kitchen, but their neighbor, Mrs. Francata.

Sarah didn't really pay attention until she heard the alarm in her mother's voice.

"Shirley," Mom said, "what's the matter?"

Then even Sarah, caught up in the joy of her parents' acceptance of Maxine, noticed Mrs. Francata's red and swollen eyes.

"He followed me home," Mrs. Francata said with a sniffle.

"Who?" Dad asked, his voice sharp with worry. "Somebody followed you from the bus stop?" Immediately he looked out the window, searching the shadows on the street.

"Not some*body*," Mrs. Francata said. She sounded all stuffy, as though she'd been crying for a long time, or as though she had a bad cold. "Something."

There was a scratching at the door, and Sarah shivered. It was, after all, Halloween night, and who knew what was out and about on such a night?

From the basement, Dudley barked.

Sounding a lot braver than Sarah felt, Justin told Mrs. Francata, "Probably just kids, trying to scare you."

"No," Mrs. Francata said, wiping her eyes with a handkerchief. "Let him in, will you?"

Let him in?

Dad hesitated, then went to the door. "Oh," he said. He held the door wide open.

A black-and-white puppy trotted in, tail wagging enthusiastically.

"He's such a friendly thing," Mrs. Francata said nasally, "but I'm terribly allergic. He followed me the two blocks from the bus stop, which was sweet, but then he sat outside my door. And he wouldn't leave. He was whimpering, and I was worried that maybe he was hurt, but I looked him all over, and I don't think he is."

He certainly didn't act like a hurt dog, Sarah thought.

Mrs. Francata said, "When I was with him, he was happy, just like he is now. But as soon as I closed the door, he began whimpering again. So I gave him a little bit of turkey casserole and a bowl of water, but he doesn't seem to be hungry—just lost. Have you children ever seen him in the neighborhood before?"

Sarah and Justin shook their heads.

"I don't think I've ever seen him before either," Mrs. Francata said. "I'm willing to put an ad in the paper so his owners can come and get him, but I can't just leave him running loose outside—at night. What if he runs in the street and gets hit by a car? But I can't keep him inside. I tried that for about half an hour, and look at me." She used her hanky to wipe her nose.

"Gee," Mom said. "That's too bad."

Sarah could see she was getting nervous.

Mrs. Francata suddenly noticed the three other puppies in the kitchen. "I knew you had a dog," she said, "so I figured you weren't allergic, but I didn't know you had so many."

"There seem to be a lot of stray puppies tonight," Mom said.

Just then the phone rang, and Dad went to answer it while Mrs. Francata said, "I can't keep him in the basement because there are too many things for him to get into there, and I can't keep him upstairs. Do you think you could keep him just for tonight? I can ask my sister tomorrow if she'll take him for a few days, but it's too late to call her now—she doesn't answer the phone after eight-thirty."

"Well . . . ," Mom said. She didn't say what Sarah was thinking, that their doorbell didn't usually ring after eight-thirty either. Mom was obviously half listening to Dad to see if anything was wrong. So was Sarah.

"Hello?" Dad said. Then, surprised: "Oh, hello, Mrs. Lynch."

Uh-oh, Sarah thought. Mrs. Lynch was her kindergarten teacher. Why would *she* be calling? Sarah tried to remember if she had done anything to get Mrs. Lynch upset today. She couldn't think of anything, besides accidentally pasting her art project to the table. But Mrs. Lynch was used to things like that.

Dad was wearing a questioning expression on his face as Mrs. Lynch told him something.

Just in case Sarah could hope that somehow this had nothing to do with her, Dad turned to look directly at her. "Really?" he asked into the phone. "Sarah?"

Mrs. Lynch must have said, *Yes, Sarah*.

"Are you sure?" Dad asked.

Apparently Mrs. Lynch was sure.

Sarah hoped the frown on his face was from concentrating.

"It's only October," he said. "Well, almost November."

Mrs. Lynch must have indicated she knew what month it was.

"Well," Dad said, "if you're sure . . . Do you need us to come in to see you? Any paperwork or anything?"

That sounded like serious trouble. Sarah hoped that whatever it was wouldn't make them mad enough to change their minds about Maxine.

Even Mrs. Francata had stopped worrying about her allergy and was listening.

"All right," Dad said. "Yes. I understand. Really, I shouldn't be surprised. Thank you for calling."

"What is it?" Mom asked as soon as Dad hung up the phone.

Justin patted Sarah's shoulder reassuringly.

"It seems," Dad said, "that Mrs. Lynch has

decided kindergarten is too easy for Sarah. She wants to move her right into first grade."

"Way to go!" Justin cheered.

Wow, Sarah thought. People *did* think she was smart after all.

"Well!" Mom said, obviously flustered.

"Isn't that nice?" Mrs. Francata said. "I'll just be leaving, because I'm sure you want to celebrate." She was about to dab at her eyes with the hanky before she remembered that she had used it on her nose, so she just put the hanky in her pocket and rubbed her eye with her finger. She looked at the black-and-white puppy, who looked back at her, tail still wagging. "Come on," she told the puppy. "I'm sure I can survive one night with you in the house."

She really didn't sound as though she could. She rummaged through the pockets of her jacket, looking for a fresh hanky, then ended by just giving a great unladylike sniffle that bordered on a snort.

"Oh," Mom said. "That's all right. I suppose we can take in one more dog for the night. At least they all seem to get along together nicely."

Mrs. Francata didn't give her a chance to change her mind. "Thank you," she said. "That's so kind of you. I'll call you tomorrow to let you know what my sister says. And meanwhile I'll call the paper to put a notice in the lost and found." She stooped down to pet the puppy. "Good-bye, little cutie," she said. "Behave yourself." She sneezed, and Dad handed her a paper towel from the counter. "Thank you," she said. And to Sarah she added, "And congratulations, you smart girl."

CHAPTER 6
When Is Halloween Like Christmas?

Sarah had not yet been able to settle down after the twin pieces of good news—that she could keep Maxine, and that she was moving up to first grade—when somebody else knocked at their door. They were all in the dining room, with the Halloween candy she and Justin had gathered spread out on the table while their parents examined it, just to be sure. Dad, as always, was doing a lot of tasting—just to be sure.

"I hope that's not Mrs. Francata with another puppy," Mom said, but her laugh was forced, as though that was exactly what she was afraid of.

Only the last part was right: Sarah saw that it was their neighbor from the other side, Mr. Niedermeier, instead of Mrs. Francata, but he *was* carrying a puppy.

"Is this yours?" he asked Mom, shoving the squirming, yipping bundle of fur at her.

"No," Mom said, not sounding as friendly as she usually did.

Mr. Niedermeier didn't seem to notice Mom's Little Bo Peep costume, or her unfriendliness, or the fact that she had said no. "Because he's been sitting under our baby's window for the last hour or so, barking his fool head off."

"I'm sorry to hear that," Mom told him, "but this is not our dog."

"You have a collie," Mr. Niedermeier said, as though he was sure Mom was trying to get away with something.

Dad joined Mom in the kitchen, while Sarah and Justin peeked in through the dining room doorway. "We have a full-grown dog that is about a quarter collie," Dad pointed out. "What you have there looks like a purebred sheltie puppy."

Mr. Niedermeier considered this, perhaps not willing to trust a man dressed like a sheep. "Not the same thing?"

Mom and Dad spoke together. "Not the same thing."

Sarah and Justin came into the kitchen to get a closer look at what was going on.

Mr. Niedermeier said, "It's only I was hoping he was yours. He doesn't have a collar."

Justin said, proudly, "Our dog, Dudley, *has* a collar."

Mr. Niedermeier sighed. "I guess I'll have to call the pound."

"Oh," Sarah said. "But he looks like such a nice puppy. You're not allergic to dogs, are you?"

"No," Mr. Niedermeier said, "as a matter of fact, we have two Pomeranians, one for me and one for my wife. Two dogs is enough for any household." He looked disapprovingly at the terrier puppy, the puppy Dad had found in his car, the black-and-white puppy, and Maxine. And at Dudley, who had finally been let up from the basement.

Sarah said, "One dog for you, and one for Mrs. Niedermeier, and a puppy for your little baby. Everybody should have a dog."

"Not a yappy one," Mr. Niedermeier said, and he left, carrying the puppy with him.

"Somebody is sure to get him from the

pound," Mom assured the family as they watched Mr. Niedermeier cross the lawn back to his house, "a purebred sheltie like that."

The door of the house across the street opened. Ms. Pizzelli-McPenney, who didn't have a husband or kids, but about a dozen cats, shooed a cocker spaniel out onto the porch with a broom. "Scat!" she said, loud enough for Sarah and her family to hear. "My cats don't like you, and I don't like you. Go back to wherever you came from."

She didn't like dogs? Sarah couldn't imagine such a thing. But there seemed to be quite a few extra dogs on their street this evening: One was napping on top of old Mr. Milano's boat that he had parked in his driveway for the winter—which old Mr. Milano wouldn't be happy to see—and one was trying to get into the garbage cans next to Mrs. Francata's garage, and one was barking at a pumpkin on somebody's porch, and two others were circling each other and growling, looking ready to fight. Had people who didn't want dogs simply refused to take in the dogs they had suddenly received?

Dad saw Sarah's sad face. "Long day," he said, closing the door. "And long past a certain little girl's bedtime. And getting close to a certain young man's bedtime, too."

"Aw, Dad," Justin said, "fairy princesses go to bed by nine, but vampires stay up all night."

"Nice try," Mom told him. "Take a shower and wash all that gunk out of your hair so it doesn't come off on your sheets."

In her room, Sarah put Maxine's box right by her own bed. She took off her tiara and her wings, put her magic wand on her dresser, and changed from her little pink top, skirt, and tights into a flannel nightie. She put the pink top in the box with Maxine—which Dad had suggested—so the little puppy could smell her and not get lonely.

But when she was ready to brush her teeth, Justin was already in the bathroom, taking a shower. Sarah sat on the edge of her bed, waiting. Now that she was ready for bed, she was sleepy. She could hear Justin singing "The Star-Spangled Banner." "He's not going to be done any time soon," she told Maxine.

Maxine, who obviously wasn't worried about brushing *her* teeth before going to bed, laid her head on her paws and yawned.

"We need another bathroom," Sarah said.

She heard her mother knock on the bathroom door. "Save some of the hot water," Mom called to Justin. "I need to wash my hair tonight, too."

"I wish we had an extra bathroom," Sarah said.

She couldn't wait any longer and decided she wasn't likely to get a mouthful of cavities from skipping just one night of brushing, so she got off the bed to pull her covers back and noticed a door between her dresser and the closet. A door that had never been there before.

Sarah pinched herself to make sure she wasn't dreaming. She picked Maxine up out of her box. "Do you see it, too?" Sarah asked.

Maxine licked her face, which was no answer at all.

"I wish dogs could talk," Sarah said.

Amazingly, Maxine spoke. What she said was, "Doors and gates. Doors and gates. I don't like doors and gates. They keep me from running where I want, they get in the way. Doors and gates. I don't know why people have them. Dogs don't have them. My mama could jump over the gate, but even she couldn't get through a closed door."

"Maxine!" Sarah cried. "You can talk."

"So can you," Maxine pointed out, scratching behind her ear.

Still, that didn't explain the puzzle of the door. Sarah would show her parents how smart Maxine was in a minute. But for the moment she set Maxine down to see if she would sniff out danger on the other side of the door or act afraid. But Maxine only said, "Oooo, what's that? I'd better chase it," and she began chasing her tail instead of investigating the door.

Sarah took a deep breath and opened the door—into a bright and clean new bathroom.

"Wow!" Sarah said. A bathroom of her own. Everything was so perfect this day. "This is just like Christmas," she said. Then, because it seemed like such a fine idea, she added, "I wish every day was Christmas."

CHAPTER 7
Fa-la-la-la-la

Rushing home from the Irondequoit Senior Center, the old witch was cranky. *The cauldron!* she thought. How could she have forgotten that the last thing she was supposed to bring for making the mulled cider wasn't another ingredient—it was the cauldron to mix it in? Three C's: Cider, cinnamon, and cauldron. The cider and the cinnamon, she needed to pick up from the supermarket; the cauldron, she was supposed to bring from home. Instead, she had gone to the store and taken a guess at the third ingredient. What she had guessed was coconut.

The other witches on the refreshments committee had laughed at her when they saw her unpacking the grocery bag. "Who ever heard of putting coconut in cider?" they hooted. But then, when they had seen that her feelings were hurt, they had tried to pretend everything was fine. "Strange—but exotic," they said. "It's better to experiment than to get into a rut," they said. "We can boil it up in the Mr. Coffee machine, and it's sure to be a hit," they said. But they also told the witch who was in charge of the tea to make extra.

Worse than the criticism was having them try so hard to be accommodating. "I can go back home and fetch the cauldron," she told them—as though she hadn't been running late enough as it was.

The old witch felt like a fool.

And besides that, she felt cold. And no wonder. It was *snowing,* for goodness' sakes. Whoever heard of snow on All Hallows' Eve?

And now, as she and her magic broom circled her backyard to make sure no one was watching, she saw that there were way too many lights on all over the neighborhood. Festive, twinkling, many-colored lights. What was going on? she wondered. If she didn't know better, she would have thought she had wandered into the Christmas season. Lights were on trees, lights glowed in windows, lights hung from eaves and bordered walkways. She saw that some people had draped strings of lights across the pumpkins on their stoops; a straw man in a lawn chair on someone's porch had tinsel hanging from him; and there were Christmas ornaments attached to the Styrofoam gravestones in someone else's yard.

Maybe the snow had put a few people into the Christmas mood—but *all* of them?

The old witch flew closer to the snow-dusted ground for a better look, and a dog started barking at her, following as though he were chasing a car. Worse yet, the dog's barking sounded like actual words. She was sure she could hear the creature saying "Gotta catch, gotta catch, gotta catch!"

The old witch was worried that this would attract attention, but then she saw that there were a lot of dogs wandering about the neighborhood.

"Let me in!" some of them barked.

"Hey! You other dogs! This street is *my* territory!" others barked.

"Sorry I peed on the rug," one repeated over and over.

"What's going on, I wonder?" the old witch said out loud.

The broom told her, "I can't say."

Against her better judgment, the witch asked, "Why not?"

"Because," the broom said, "I'm not the kind of cleaning device that goes around saying 'I told you so.'"

The old witch considered this for a moment. Her broom was *exactly* the kind of cleaning device that would say "I told you so." But she didn't argue. "You think this has something to do with that little girl I gave wishes to this evening?"

"I can't say," the broom told her again in its self-satisfied voice.

The witch landed the broom in her backyard, despite the drifts of snow and the barking dog. There were enough other dogs barking and fussing that she doubted anybody would notice. And as soon as the broom stopped moving, the chasing dog lost interest and took off after a low-flying airplane, repeating "Gotta catch."

The old witch shook her head. What was going on? It was October thirty-first. Even so, a group of Christmas carolers dressed like a mummy, a gypsy, a train engineer, and a Hershey's Kiss strolled from door to door singing "Good King Wenceslas." A Doberman pinscher—a real one, not someone in costume—was with them, and he sang also. But he didn't sing very well; he was loud and off-key and kept forgetting the words, howling "Fa-la-la-la-la" whenever he lost track.

The old witch sighed, knowing the broom was probably right. This mixing of Halloween and Christmas, and the overabundance of dogs—not to mention talking, singing dogs—was too strange to be anything besides the result of her hasty decision to grant wishes to a little girl. Who knew what else that little girl could have wished for that might cause all sorts of problems?

Because it would take too much time to track down every bit of magic the little girl had performed with her magic wand, the old witch decided the easiest thing to do would be a reversal spell.

"Brace yourself," the witch warned the broom.

"Just be careful—," the broom started as the old witch let loose a wave of magic. Too late.

Quicker than a sigh, time began to rewind at high speed: The snow undrifted from people's yards and retreated back up into the sky; the moon faded and dipped away; people and animals scurried along backward on the streets and sidewalks until the sun returned to just below the horizon—to a point in time before the Christmas decorations had been prematurely unpacked from attics, closets, and basements, and when trick-or-treaters rather than talking dogs roamed the neighborhood; to a point in time just after the old witch bespelled the little girl's plastic wand. Beyond *that* point, the magic could not get.

The broom sighed. "I can't believe you did a simple reversal spell." It added, "Just remember that I'm too big to say 'I told you so' about the things I told you so about."

"Yeah, yeah," the witch said, and waited to see what would happen now that Sarah's wishes would all turn backward.

CHAPTER 8
Witch Wish #2

Sarah was having trouble keeping up with Justin as they circled around the supermarket and headed down the next street to do their trick-or-treating. "You're walking too fast," she told him. "You're going to make me fall."

"It would serve you right," Justin said. "And then I could bring you back home and go out with my friends instead of my baby sister. What's the matter with you? Talking to a stranger—to a bag lady! That's just dumb."

"I wish you'd be nice to me," Sarah muttered.

Sarah had a sensation somewhere between hearing and feeling, like a cork being twisted out of a bottle, but inside her bones.

Justin stopped so suddenly, Sarah bumped into him. "You're a rotten, useless, little kid," he said, which was meaner than he'd ever been before. "I hate being stuck with you."

His words were so harsh and so unexpected, Sarah started to cry.

"And you're a crybaby, too," Justin said. "Here, I'll give you something to cry about." He reached into her bag of candy and took a couple of handfuls of it for himself. "And if you tell Mom and Dad, I'll make sure you're even sorrier later."

Sarah tried to stop sniffling so that he wouldn't take any more of her candy, and she began to hiccup. She held her breath and swallowed, and the next hiccup came out even louder, sounding like a burp.

As though *he* had never burped, Justin said, "And you're disgusting, too."

"I'd stop if I could," she told him. "I wish my hiccups would go away."

Again she had the sensation of something she could barely hear and almost feel, but the hiccups didn't go away. In fact, they came faster and louder.

"Wonderful," Justin muttered.

They'd reached the first house after the store. Justin rang the bell, and as soon as the woman who lived there opened the door, he held his cape out, blocking Sarah from view, and said, "I vant to drink your blood."

"Oooo, spooky!" the lady said. She had a bowl of suckers, and she said, "I imagine you want a bloodred one."

Peeking over Justin's extended arm, Sarah saw Justin lick his lips in exaggerated delight. "Blood," he said in his fake accent, "it's my favorite color."

"Trick—," Sarah started, but she had waited to be between hiccups, and she waited too long. The woman never saw her and shut the door. Sarah stood on the step and hiccupped.

Flapping his cape, Justin ran across the lawn to the next door.

Sarah considered whether she should ring the sucker lady's doorbell on her own, but she was sure Justin wouldn't wait for her. Mean though he was being tonight, she didn't want to get separated from him and be out alone.

But she never exactly caught up, all the way down the street. If she stopped for candy, Justin kept right on going. She skipped houses when he got too far ahead of her, but he could move faster than she could, with his long legs and his ability to jump over obstacles. Sarah, who was unable to jump over bushes and un-willing to risk landing on flower beds, had to keep going back out to the sidewalk while Justin could cut across lawns.

"Can I have some for my sister?" she heard him ask over and over, and he would point back to her. But then he put the candy in his own pillowcase bag.

After skipping a bunch of houses, she had finally joined Justin at one door when a dog jumped out at them.

Startled, Sarah squealed. Justin leaped back, leaving Sarah as dog bait. Scares can some-times frighten hiccups right out of you, Sarah knew, but in this case, she kept on hiccupping.

"That's okay," the home owner said. "Daisy's just saying hello. She wouldn't hurt you. Get down, Daisy."

Daisy was wagging her tail, and hesitantly Sarah put her hand out. Daisy licked it, which was tickly.

"Down," Daisy's owner repeated, and the dog lay down.

Justin rejoined Sarah on the stairs.

The man said, "Don't be afraid. She won't bite."

"I'm not afraid," Justin said.

Sarah was—a little—but she put her hand out anyway, to pet the beautiful dog. Daisy's fur was soft.

From inside the house, Sarah heard a whimper. She looked up and saw a bunch of puppies leaning on a baby gate, which came down with a bang under their weight. In a moment the puppies were running across the living room toward them.

"Uh-oh," the owner said, not sounding truly worried. "The puppies knocked the gate down again."

The puppies—there were seven of them—swarmed over Daisy and onto the stoop, sniffing and licking at Sarah and Justin.

"Oh, they're so cute," Sarah said.

"Want one?" the man asked. "We're looking for homes for them."

Wow! Sarah thought.

But Justin shook his head. "We already have a dog," he told the man.

"But Dudley is *your* dog," Sarah protested.

"Duh!" Justin said. "You're not old enough or smart enough to have your own dog."

"I want a dog of my own," Sarah said.

"Go ahead, ask Mom," Justin sneered at her. "She'll only say no." Justin seemed to warm up to the idea. "Go ahead," he repeated. "Take one. You're going to be in so much trouble—this I've got to see." He leaned close to whisper into her ear, "They're ugly anyway, and they all look brain-damaged."

"Everyone should have a dog," Sarah said. "I wish everyone did."

There was that noise again—strange but familiar—and she stumbled on the stoop, even though there was nothing there, certainly nothing to trip her.

"Get away from me, you spaz," Justin said, shoving her away.

"What was that sound?" she asked.

The man whose house it was glanced around, looking a bit confused, and asked, "What sound?"

Justin ignored the man and jeered at Sarah, "Do you mean your hiccupping?"

"No," Sarah said. "It sounded sort of squeaky— like two balloons rubbing against each other."

"Well, then, duh," Justin said. "Just as a guess, maybe it was two balloons rubbing against each other. *Duh.*"

But I wouldn't have felt that in my teeth, Sarah thought.

She looked at the man, who was scratching his head, looking around as though he'd lost something. Sarah felt she should know what he'd lost, and she looked down, but there wasn't anything on the stoop. "I was sure . . . ," he started, but then he drifted off, "Oh, well." He reached over to the table by the door and handed out two candy bars, one for Justin and one for Sarah.

"Thanks," Sarah said, then, *"Hic!"* as Justin flapped his way across the lawn over to the next house.

The man closed the door, but Sarah heard him call, "Daisy? Daisy? Where'd you go, girl?"

Daisy, Sarah thought. Now where had she heard that name before?

Justin leaped out of the bushes at her. Startled, she dropped both her pillowcase of candy and her flashlight. The flashlight cracked open and the light went out. Justin picked up the pillowcase and ran down the street, cackling a loud, mad-scientist cackle.

Sarah continued to hiccup. She walked slowly because of the dark.

When it became obvious she'd never catch up to Justin, she joined another group of trick-or-treaters: a pirate, a clown, two kids dressed up as a cow—which was a neat costume, but they had trouble coordinating their back and front ends. Neither end seemed to mind that Sarah couldn't stop hiccupping.

"I love Halloween," the front end of the cow said as a woman handed out coupons for free ice-cream cones at the corner dairy.

"*Hic!* Me too," Sarah said, even though she knew she could only go to as many houses as she could carry the treats in her hands. But she was getting caught up in the excitement now that Justin was gone. "I—*hic!*—wish every day was Halloween."

She felt a sensation that made her finger-nails tingle, and at the same time there was a squeegee-on-glass sound.

The woman who'd answered the door said, "Yes? May I help you?"

Sarah glanced around to see if somebody else would answer, but she was all alone. How had she gotten here? She couldn't remember why she'd come to this house. And for some reason she found herself surprised to be wearing her jeans and her blue-and-purple-striped sweatshirt. Even though it was her favorite outfit, she felt something was missing. She touched her head, but there was nothing there. And why, she wondered, was she holding a stick to which someone had glued a star and streamers?

"Are you lost?" the woman asked Sarah.

"No," Sarah said. "I know my way home." She hiccupped.

"Good." The woman sounded relieved. "Do you need a drink of water?"

Sarah shook her head.

"Then you'd better be going home now. It's too late for such a little girl to be out ringing people's doorbells."

Sarah thought so, too. Still hiccupping, she walked to her own house.

"Thank goodness you're home," her mother called from the kitchen. "What were you doing out so late? I was worried."

Worried, Sarah knew, sometimes grew into long lectures and even longer timeouts. As she closed the front door behind her, Sarah whispered, "I wish Mom and Dad weren't so excitable."

The door—or something—squeaked, rattling a spot between Sarah's eyes.

Sarah walked into the kitchen and found her mother sitting at the kitchen table with Justin. Justin was doing his homework and smirking at her. Her mother was tapping her foot and shaking her finger at Sarah. "You, young lady," her mother said, "are in serious trouble."

CHAPTER 9
Missing

"What were you thinking," Mom demanded, "wandering off like that?"

Sarah hiccupped before she could speak. She said, "I don't know."

"Your father is driving around the neighborhood looking for you. That was very naughty of you to worry us like that."

"Yeah," Justin said. "And what did you do with Dudley?"

"Dudley?" Sarah repeated.

"Duh," Justin said. "Big collie that's lived here longer than you have—I'm sure you must have noticed him."

"Dudley—*hic!*—your dog," Sarah said. "I

know who he is. I don't know why you're asking me about him."

"Because he's gone. Did you let him out of the yard? You did, didn't you? And now he's run away. He's lost, because of you."

"And you were worried that we'd reprimand you," Mom finished, "and that's why you decided to run away from home."

"I didn't run away from home," Sarah protested. *"Hic!"*

At that point, they heard Dad's car pull into the driveway.

"It's all right, Sarah," Mom told her. "You just need to own up to your mistakes, and tell the truth. That's the important thing, telling the truth."

Justin cut in, saying, "The important thing is that Dudley is lost, and it's Sarah's fault. It'd be better if we still had Dudley and Sarah was the one who was lost."

"Justin, that's enough," Mom said. "Sarah, take a drink of water."

Sarah did. It didn't do any good.

Dad came in through the side door, saying, *"There* you are. You led us on a merry chase, young lady. You'd better have a very good explanation."

"I don't have any explanation," Sarah said between hiccups. "I don't remember where I've been."

"Sarah," Dad warned.

"Just tell the truth," Mom said. "And take another drink of water."

"That *is* the truth," Sarah insisted. She took some more water. "*Hic!* I wish everyone would believe me."

And even as she heard that oddly familiar sound that seemed to come from inside her, deeper even than the hiccups, she heard Mom, Dad, and Justin speak as though with one voice: "Well, we don't."

"It's true," Sarah insisted. "*Hic!* I just all of a sudden found myself one street over. *Hic!* I don't know how or why."

Justin muttered, "The rubber band that keeps her brain working must suddenly have snapped."

"Did not," Sarah said.

"Did too," Justin argued. "All kindergartners have brains that run on rubber-band power. That's why they're all so dumb."

Mom ignored him. "Sarah," she said in her quiet but no-nonsense voice, "you're not being reasonable."

Not being reasonable. That's what her parents said whenever they didn't like what she said.

She turned on her heel and headed down the hall to her room, stamping her feet. "I am *not* an unreasonable dummy," she muttered to herself. She was smart enough not to let Dudley escape out of the yard, and she was smart enough to know the truth—and the truth was something weird had happened that had caused her to lose track of time and make her forget where she'd been. Maybe it had something to do with the stick decorated to look like a magic wand, or maybe it didn't. In any case, she muttered to herself, "I wish people thought I was smart."

There was a sound—could it have been the squeak of a rubber band?—that she felt right down to her toes. But nobody else seemed to hear it. "Young lady," her mother called after her, "don't you dare stamp your feet and slam your door. You get back here until we finish talking with you. Do you understand me?"

Sarah stamped her feet all the way back up the hall. She stood there and hiccupped, not even trying to make the sound smaller.

Her father said, "I don't think she understands." He looked at Sarah and spoke very slowly and very earnestly, as though she were a baby: "Sarah was very naughty to make her parents worry. Doesn't Sarah want to be a good girl? Good girls tell the truth. Does Sarah understand?"

Her mother had her hands on her hips. "We can take anything but lying."

"I'm not lying!" Sarah said. "I don't know anything about Dudley, and I don't know where I've been."

"Dog thief!" Justin taunted.

Luckily he was interrupted by someone knocking on the door.

"And take a drink of water," Dad ordered over his shoulder as he went to see who it was.

Sarah sincerely hoped it was someone with good news rather than more trouble.

But she doubted it.

CHAPTER 10
A Likely Story . . .

The person at their door was their neighbor, Mrs. Francata. She looked as though she'd been crying.

"Shirley," Mom said, "what's the matter?"

"Oh, I know it's silly to be upset about such a thing when there's so much real trouble in the world, but I just had a call from my sister who says someone's stolen their dog. Can you imagine? Why would somebody be so mean? And such a nice dog it was, too." Mrs. Francata gave a sniffle.

"Who stole it?" Dad asked. He glanced out the window, as though to make sure there were no dognappers here on this street.

"Nobody knows," Mrs. Francata said. She sounded all stuffy from crying. "The thing is, someone must have broken into their house, because that's where the dog was."

"Yeah, well, their dog isn't the only dog that's gone," Justin said. "Except we know who's responsible for our dog being missing."

Dad told Mrs. Francata, "Maybe someone left the door open, and your sister's dog just escaped. Maybe he wasn't stolen; he's just lost."

"I bet it was Sarah," Justin said. "She's the one who left *our* gate open."

"It wasn't me," Sarah protested.

Nobody seemed to believe anything she said tonight. "Sarah!" Mrs. Francata cried. "How could you!"

"I didn't," Sarah said. "I don't even know— *Hic!*—your sister or where she lives."

Mrs. Francata only shook her head and went "Tsk!"

Just then the phone rang. Dad went to answer it while Mrs. Francata said, "Do you belong to a band of dog thieves, Sarah, or did you just let the dogs go? I myself am allergic to dogs, but I don't think people should go around stealing them. I have half a mind to call the police."

"Oh," Mom said, "maybe we should wait to see if your sister's dog finds its way back by morning. Sarah is so young to be in trouble with the police. She really doesn't understand what she's done." Sarah could tell Mom was only half listening to Mrs. Francata; she was also half listening to Dad to see if anything else was wrong. Sarah listened, too, between hiccups.

"Hello?" Dad said. His voice switched from concerned to surprised: "Oh, hello, Mrs. Lynch."

Dad was frowning, but Sarah hoped that was because he was concentrating. He turned to look directly at her. "Really?" he asked into the phone. "Sarah? Are you sure?"

After another moment, Dad said, "It's only October. Well, almost November."

Another pause.

"Well," Dad said, "if you're sure . . . Do you need us to come in to see you? Any paperwork or anything?"

Another pause.

"All right," Dad said. "Yes. I understand. Really, I shouldn't be surprised. Thank you for calling."

"What is it?" Mom asked as soon as Dad hung up the phone.

Justin stuck his tongue out at Sarah.

"It seems," Dad said, "that Mrs. Lynch has decided that Sarah needs to be sent back to prekindergarten."

How embarrassing! Sarah knew that sometimes kids had to repeat a grade, but she'd never heard of anyone actually being sent back a year. She groaned out loud and whispered to herself, "I hope nobody hears about this." She heard that cork or rubber band squeak, and felt it in her earlobes.

"Way to go!" Justin hooted. "Sarah flunked kindergarten after only two months!"

"Well!" Mom said, obviously flustered. "What did you *do,* Sarah?"

"I bet she stole the teacher's dog, too," Justin said.

"I didn't do anything," Sarah said. "Well, except I accidentally glued my art project to the table. But that happens to a lot of kids. *Hic!*"

"A likely story," Mrs. Francata said. "You have until noon to return my sister's dog before I go to the police with what I know. I'll just be leaving now." She patted Sarah's mother on the hand. "And as far as the kindergarten thing goes, some children just need a longer start than others, dearie. I'm sure once you get the thieving straightened out, she won't have to repeat too many grades." But her look said she doubted that Sarah was smart enough to recognize her own name. "And, Sarah," she added, "take a drink of water, will you?"

CHAPTER 11
On the Spot

Things were just going from bad to worse: Justin—who normally was a pretty good brother—just got meaner and meaner, her parents wouldn't believe anything she said, she had just been demoted to nursery school— what more could happen? When somebody else knocked at their door, Sarah knew it would be more bad news.

It was Mr. Niedermeier, asking whether anybody had seen his two Pomeranians, who had disappeared from the house. Through the open door, they could hear other people roaming up and down the street, calling out to their dogs.

"I don't know what to make of this," Mr. Niedermeier said. "Our dogs were perfectly well behaved. Even if someone was trying to get rid of all nuisance dogs, why would they want to get rid of ours?"

Sarah couldn't imagine such a thing either. She knew she didn't have anything to do with the dogs disappearing, so who did?

Luckily, Mom clapped her hand over Justin's mouth before he could blame Sarah. It wasn't, Sarah knew, that Mom believed her—she just was too ashamed to want everyone to know.

But dogs weren't all Mr. Niedermeier wanted to talk about. "So," Mr. Niedermeier said, "I understand your little girl, Sarah, is being sent back to nursery school."

From beneath Mom's hand, Justin made a snorting sound.

Dad groaned. "How did you hear about that?"

"My sister's the principal at Iroquois School. She just called to let me know. She said that in all her years in education she's never had to move a student back like that before."

"Imagine," Mom said faintly.

"Well, good luck to you, kid," Mr. Niedermeier told Sarah. He shook his head sadly. "You'll need it, poor thing."

Closing the door after Mr. Niedermeier, Dad

said, "It's been a long day. Sarah, I want you to think about what you've done, understand? First thing tomorrow morning, you better be ready to explain where those dogs are."

Sarah knew it was no use arguing.

Dad said, "And it's getting close to a certain young man's bedtime, too."

"Aw, Dad," Justin said, "pre-K kids go to bed by nine, but fifth graders can stay up longer."

"Nice try," Mom told him. "Both of you, off to bed."

In her bedroom, Sarah put on her flannel nightie. But just as she was ready to brush her teeth, Justin ran down the hall ahead of her and slammed the bathroom door in her face. "I'll only be an hour or two," he called out to her. He made rude noises that she recognized was just blowing air onto his wrist but which was meant to sound as though he were having a major attack of gas. Then she heard him turn on the shower. Sarah sat on the edge of her bed, waiting. And waiting. And waiting.

From downstairs, she heard her father turn on the TV. The news was on, and the news-caster's voice was saying, "This just in: It has been brought to our attention that six-year-old

Sarah Gonnella of Iroquois School in Irondequoit is being sent back to prekindergarten after flunking out of kindergarten, a first for our school district. Reporter DeeDee Hampton is on the scene now."

Sarah hoped they meant at the school, but just at that moment the doorbell rang.

"Don't—" she heard her father call out, but it was too late: Sarah heard Mom open the door.

"Good evening, ma'am. Channel Twelve On-the-Spot News here. Are you the mother of Sarah Gonnella?"

Mom must have slammed the door shut. The reporter rang the doorbell again, then knocked on the door. "Do you have a statement?" the reporter shouted through the door.

"Go away!" Mom said.

Sarah heard Dad moan, "This is so embarrassing. The guys on my bowling team will never let me live this down."

Sarah continued sitting on her bed, waiting for Justin to finish in the bathroom.

She heard a noise outside her window at the same time Dad bellowed, "Sarah!" She looked up in time to see a man with a video camera. A woman with a microphone motioned for Sarah to open the window. From the TV in the living room, Sarah heard the woman announce, "The image on your screens now—"

Mom came running down the hall and into Sarah's room. "Go away!" she shouted to the reporters outside, and she pulled the curtains closed. Through glass and curtain Sarah heard the woman say, "But we've got a link with the network. You could be on 'Sixty Minutes.'"

Mom shook her head and left to check all the other window locks.

Still Sarah waited for Justin to finish his shower. "We need another bathroom," Sarah said to herself. She wanted to go to sleep and wake up tomorrow and have everything back to normal.

"I wish we had an extra bathroom," Sarah said.

She heard a noise that might have been Justin rubbing something against the wet tiles in the bathroom, but it sounded closer. And it made the ends of her hair itch.

Out in the hall, Mom said, "That's odd."

"What?" Sarah asked.

Mom leaned into Sarah's room, glanced around, then left.

"What?" Sarah repeated.

She heard the hall closet door open, then close.

Sarah stepped out into the hall.

Justin was standing there dripping soapy lather, a towel around his waist, looking dazed. Mom rapped her knuckles along the wall of the hallway as though trying to find a hollow spot.

"What's the matter?" Sarah asked.

Mom opened, then closed, the door to the attic. "We seem," she said, "to have misplaced the bathroom."

A bright light flooded the house, despite the fact that Mom had pulled all the curtains tight. And there was a strange *whup! whup! whup!* noise that seemed to be settling on the house from above.

"What's that?" Sarah asked, frightened.

Dad came running down the hall. "News helicopters," he shouted to be heard above the racket, "landing in the backyard. Someone's got spotlights, directing them in here."

Sarah peeled the curtain back from her window, just a bit for a peek. There were, indeed, spotlights shining on their house, and some aimed up in the sky, like for a grand opening. A technician was setting up a sound system, and was repeating "Sarah Gonnella, Sarah

Gonnella" as he worked on cranking up the volume from very loud to extremely loud. Someone had used the side of Mrs. Francata's garage as a billboard to put up a sign, for which Sarah's kindergarten picture had been blown up to a size of six feet wide and eight feet tall. The sign said:

SARAH GONNELLA,

KINDERGARTEN FAILURE.

KIDS, DON'T LET THIS HAPPEN TO YOU.

CHAPTER 12
Let's Try Again

The old witch had needed to go to the supermarket again, because the cider, cinnamon, and coconut she had bought earlier in the evening had disappeared once she made the evening go back to the moment when she'd enchanted Sarah's toy magic wand.

This time she remembered the only items she needed to buy were cider and cinnamon.

It was only when she returned to her house to fetch her cauldron that she realized she should also have bought a fishbowl for Sweet Pea, since he couldn't stay in the cauldron while she mulled the cider.

After looking all through her cupboards and not finding anything suitable to hold the goldfish, she finally had to use the gravy boat she had bought at a home decorating party that spring. "Just for this evening," she assured Sweet Pea.

Sweet Pea didn't say anything. He never did.

The old witch dumped the water out of the cauldron down the bathtub drain.

"Are we going to make a toxic brew?" the cauldron asked sleepily. It pretty much slept between batches of toxic brew.

"This is the twenty-first century," the old witch reminded. "Nobody makes toxic brew anymore."

"No kidding," the broom grumbled, though nobody had been talking to it. "Nobody does much of anything anymore."

"I could use you to sweep up the bat droppings in the attic," the witch warned.

"The bats have flown south for the winter," the broom answered, though that had nothing to do with anything. It hated to let anyone else get the last word.

The witch hung the empty cauldron from the end of the broom, tucked under one arm the grocery bag with the cider and cinnamon, and started off for the senior center, knowing she had just enough time to get there before her sister witches would make fun of her for always being late. Still, she couldn't help but notice all the lights several streets over.

"Probably nothing to do with us," she said out loud.

"Oh, my, no," the broom said so firmly she knew she'd better go for a closer look.

When she saw the spotlights and the news helicopter and the traffic jam in front of the garage bearing the billboard likeness of Sarah, she sighed.

"Well," the old witch said, "I think this has gone quite far enough."

The broom was humming an annoying little tune to itself, but it stopped long enough to say, in a very superior tone, "I can't say."

"Oh, hush!" the witch warned. "You can be replaced by a vacuum cleaner, you know."

"Hmph!" the broom said. "You'd need a very long extension cord."

The witch saw that there was no simple way to fix the problem. Since she couldn't undo her own spell granting Sarah's magic wand the power to grant wishes, and since reversing Sarah's wishes hadn't worked, she'd have to go through Sarah's wishes spell by spell.

First, she made herself invisible.

"Now you have to be extra quiet," she reminded the broom.

"Pardon me for breathing," the broom said.

"And you go back to being a fishbowl," she told the cauldron.

"It's better than being a flowerpot," the cauldron said, showing a much better outlook on life than the broom had.

Then, once more the old witch rolled time back.

CHAPTER 13
Witch Wish #3

Standing invisibly next to Sarah and Justin, the old witch heard Sarah say, "You're walking too fast. You're going to make me fall."

"It would serve you right," Justin told her. "And then I could bring you back home and go out with my friends instead of my baby sister. What's the matter with you? Talking to a stranger—to a bag lady! That's just dumb."

"I wish you'd be nice to me," Sarah muttered.

First wish, and already the witch was unsure what to do. She didn't want to meddle with someone's very nature, especially if this was just normal brother/sister bickering. She made the wish slip away without letting the magic wand grant it.

Justin continued, "It's dangerous to talk to strangers."

"Okay," Sarah said.

"Don't do it again."

"Okay," Sarah repeated.

"All right," Justin said. "I'm sorry I made you drop that candy back there behind the store." He didn't offer to replace it, but that would have been expecting too much.

At the next house Justin rang the doorbell, then said to the woman who answered the door, "I vant to drink your blood."

"Trick or treat," Sarah chimed in a moment later.

"Oh, aren't you cute," the woman told both of them. Holding out a bowl of suckers, she asked, "Red, green, yellow, or purple?"

"Red," both Sarah and Justin answered.

"Oh, dear, there's only one red one left," the woman said, pawing through the bowl.

Both children waited expectantly. "Purple is close to red," the woman said, and dropped suckers into the kids' bags too fast for anybody to see who got what.

Door to door the two kids and the invisible witch went, with Sarah not making any more wishes until they were at the house of a man who had a dog and several puppies. "Everyone should have a dog," Sarah said. "I wish everyone did."

The man already seemed inclined to give Sarah one in any case, and the witch dissolved the wish.

"Listen," the man said, "why don't you take one of the puppies home to show your mom? If she says no, then you can bring the pup back." He winked at Sarah. "It'll be easier to talk her into it if you already have one."

Justin told him, "Our parents might not be happy."

"I'll give you my name and address and phone number," the man said. "That way your parents can contact me if they want to."

Sarah chose a puppy and said, "I'm going to call her Maxine."

The man provided a cardboard box to carry the puppy, and, true to his word, a business card—"Just in case," he said. "But good luck."

Justin carried Sarah's pillowcase of candy for her. Though he munched from her bag, he didn't complain about how long the walk home took; and he shone his flashlight on the sidewalk so that Sarah wouldn't trip.

They saw other trick-or-treaters along the way, and Sarah, excited, said, "This is such fun. I love Halloween. I wish every day was Halloween."

The old witch definitely undid that wish.

She walked with them right up to and into their own house. She held tightly to the broom so that she wouldn't accidentally knock over anything.

"Trick or treat," Sarah called.

"Welcome back," the children's mother said. She was dressed like Little Bo Peep and she used the hook end of her shepherd's crook to bring Justin closer. She kissed the top of his head before adding, "I just sent your father out to the grocery store to get more goodies. Now we can use some of the stuff you collected if anybody comes before he gets back."

"Aw, Mom," Justin complained.

"You can't give this away," Sarah said before her mother could hook her. She plunked the box containing Maxine the puppy onto the kitchen floor. Maxine started jumping at the side of the box, trying to get out.

Another dog, a big mixed breed that probably had some collie in its background, came and sniffed at the new puppy.

"Get back, Dudley," Justin said.

But apparently Dudley was about as good at following orders as a certain magic broom was.

"Oh, dear," the mother said as dog and puppy sniffed each other. "Where did you get that?"

"Some man gave him to me as a Halloween treat," Sarah said.

"That wasn't a very responsible thing to do," the mother pointed out. "He had no right to do such a thing without checking to see if it was all right with the family."

"He said we could bring her back if you said so," Sarah said. "But can't I keep her, please? Her name is Maxine. She's a very well-behaved puppy, and I promise to take care of her and feed her and walk her and clean up her poop."

Justin handed his mother the man's business card. "He's willing to take her back," he said. "If you're willing to break Sarah's heart."

"Thanks a lot for your help," his mother grumbled.

Justin grinned. "And Dudley seems to approve."

"That's not the point," the mother said. "I don't plan to get in the habit of leaving family decisions to Dudley." She held up her hand to keep either of the children from saying anything. "Your father's home."

As though he sensed somebody else in the room, Dudley started sniffing at where the old witch was standing. She made shooing gestures with her gown and broom.

The broom whispered, "Oh, wonderful. Now I'm a dog swatter. That's a very fulfilling career move for a household tool."

The witch shook the broom to get it to be quiet.

Fortunately, the family were all greeting the father, and Dudley was the kind of dog who could easily be distracted.

The father was wearing what was probably supposed to be a sheep costume and carrying a grocery bag full of enough candy to serve a small village. He'd already opened a bag of marshmallow pumpkins and was chewing on one of them. "What have you got there?" he asked Sarah.

"A puppy," Sarah said. "Her name is Maxine. Can I keep her, please, please, can I?"

The mother said, "We'll need to think about

this, and the grown-ups will discuss it on their own."

"No fair!" Sarah protested. "I can keep Maxine in my room. I'll take care of her. You won't even know she's there."

"Sarah—," the father started, but Sarah seemed to assume the worst. "Why not? Why does Justin get to have a dog and I don't?"

"Justin is older than you," the mother said, "and he knows how to take care of his dog on his own."

"But I can take care of mine," Sarah insisted. "She won't be any trouble. When I go to school, I can bring her with me. She'll be good and she won't bark or chew on things or anything. Will you, Maxine?"

"Sarah," the mother said, "you're not being reasonable."

Sarah picked the puppy up and headed for her room, stamping her feet as she left.

Luckily the witch was fast enough to keep up, so she heard Sarah mutter to herself, "I wish people thought I was smart. I wish my parents would let me keep Maxine."

Two wishes in a row. The witch already thought Sarah was just about as smart as a six-year-old should be, and she suspected Sarah's parents thought so, too, so she made the wish evaporate. And it would be dangerous to enchant the family into accepting the dog if they didn't want it and resented it, so she made that wish go away, too.

"Young lady," the children's mother said, "don't you dare stamp your feet and slam your door. You get back here until we finish talking with you."

Still stamping, Sarah returned.

"We'll think about it," the mother told Sarah. "Just for a day or two to start. We'll see how well behaved this dog of yours is. We'll see if taking care of her is as easy as you think it'll be, and if you're as responsible as you need to be."

"Thank you, thank you." Sarah hugged both her parents.

So far, the witch thought, everyone was happy, and the magic wand hadn't even granted any wishes.

A neighbor came, a woman who began sniffling and sneezing as soon as she came near the dogs, but she only wanted to borrow candy because she had run out.

Then the phone rang, which was Sarah's teacher asking for a volunteer parent to help chaperone a field trip to the museum.

And then another neighbor came to complain about the older kids who were trick-or-treating too late in the evening, ringing the doorbell and causing his dogs to bark, which kept waking up his baby.

"Speaking about how late it is," Sarah's father said after this second neighbor had left, "it's been a long day. And it's long past a certain little girl's bedtime. And getting close to a certain young man's bedtime, too."

"Aw, Dad," Justin said, "fairy princesses go to bed by nine, but vampires stay up all night."

"Nice try," the mother said. "Take a shower and wash all that gunk out of your hair so it doesn't come off on your sheets."

The old witch followed Sarah to her room, where she watched Sarah put the new puppy's box beside her own bed, using the little pink top she'd been wearing as a puppy blanket. She placed the magic wand on the dresser.

The old witch yawned. This was the third time tonight she'd stayed up past her usual bedtime, and she hadn't even made it to her party yet. Now she had to wait with Sarah for her brother to finish in the shower.

After a while, Sarah said, "I wish we had an extra bathroom."

Don't we all? the witch thought.

She couldn't let that wish get fulfilled, but she did make the hot water run out to speed Justin up.

Still, by the time Justin got out of the bathroom, Sarah had fallen asleep.

The old witch pulled the covers up over her, and she pulled the puppy's cover up over *her*. She waved the magic wand over both of them. "Sweet dreams," she wished.

CHAPTER 14
Ghastly Gala A-go-go

Outside, the old witch returned herself and the broom to visibility.

"Pleased with yourself?" the broom asked.

"Yes," the witch said.

Once again she went to the supermarket to buy cider and cinnamon, and—this time—a fishbowl for Sweet Pea. Once again she emptied the cauldron down the bathtub drain, but—since she was running even later than the other two times—she didn't have a chance to scrub the cauldron clean.

Oh, well, she thought, Sweet Pea is a very clean fish.

At the senior center, the preparation committee witches made a fuss about how late she was and how there wasn't enough time to mull the cider properly. But once it was midnight and the party officially started and people began drinking the cider, they all agreed it was as good as ever—even better than ever. The old witch smiled and said, "Thank you," and thought it best not to offer any explanations, even when they put her in charge of bringing pineapple punch for their next event, the Midwinter Hawaiian Luau.

The gala was a success, with witches and monsters who didn't normally see much of one another during the year having a chance to talk and laugh together, catching up, comparing spells, eating and dancing.

The witch, who was not much for dancing herself, encouraged her broom to join in when Jeremy the werewolf called for the guests to form a conga line. They danced from room to room of the senior center—not as wild as those years the party fell on the night of a full moon, when Jeremy would be in wolf shape and would lead the line under tables and onto the roof to howl at the moon—but fun nonetheless. One of the other witches brought her two bats, and when the conga dance was over, they volunteered to hold the broom aloft as a limbo stick for guests to dance under. Whenever someone came along whom the broom or one of the bats didn't care for, they would let the broom bounce off that guest's head.

Finally the cider was gone, the cookies—even the low-fat ones—were gone, everyone's feet were tired from dancing, their throats tired from talking, and, outside, the sky was turning pink from the sun being just about ready to peek over the edge of the world. The old witch congratulated herself for not getting stuck on the cleanup committee.

"Where are we going?" the broom asked as they walked, for it was too close to morning for flying. The witch was carrying the big cauldron by its handle, looking like a trick-or-treater with grand expectations. The broom pointed out, "Home is the other way, and I, for one, have been on my feet for too many hours."

"I'm going to the supermarket first," the old witch said.

"You wanted to get more coconut?" the broom asked in a catty tone.

"I want housewares," the witch said as she parked the broom, with the cauldron hanging from it, in the bicycle rack in the supermarket's parking lot. It wasn't until after she'd already gone inside and was in the aisle that included, among other things, vacuum cleaner bags, that she remembered their earlier conversation, when she'd threatened she might consider getting a vacuum cleaner to replace the broom.

She knew the broom had been worrying when, as she came out of the supermarket several minutes later, it greeted her by saying, "That bag's not big enough for a vacuum cleaner."

"It's big enough for a Dustbuster," the witch said, "which is a battery-driven portable vacuum cleaner." But then she took pity on the broom. "But in fact," she said, "this is a new alarm clock. I would never replace you."

The broom took her reassurance as a peace offering. "Not that I'm saying yes, or anyway, not definitely," the broom said, obviously reluctant to get to the point about something or other, "but just in case somehow—or maybe *somehow* isn't exactly the right word, but, still, if there were such a case as, one way or another—"

"*What?*" the old witch demanded.

The broom finished in a rush, "If I happened to have accidentally knocked your alarm clock off your dresser, and if that's why it doesn't work properly, I'm sorry."

"Hmm," the witch said. "I see."

"Not that I necessarily know anything about it," the broom added.

"But if you *did* do it, you'd be sorry?" the witch asked.

"Yes," the broom admitted.

"And if you were sorry, I'd forgive you," the witch said.

"Which would be nice to know," the broom said, "in case."

And so they went home to rest their feet, to warm some cocoa in the cauldron, and to tell Sweet Pea all about their adventures.